NOTES FOR PARENTS

* Point to the words as you read them, then talk
  about the pictures together.

* What is happening in the pictures? Encourage
  your toddler to comment on the people and things
  he/she recognises.

* What happens in *your* toddler's day?

Geraldine Taylor, Reading Consultant

Acknowledgment:
The publishers would like to thank Lynn Breeze for the cover illustration.

Ladybird books are widely available, but in case of
difficulty may be ordered by post or telephone from:

Ladybird Books – Cash Sales Department
Littlegate Road Paignton Devon TQ3 3BE
Telephone 0803 554761

A catalogue record for this book is available
from the British Library

Published by Ladybird Books Ltd Loughborough Leicestershire UK
Ladybird Books Inc Auburn Maine 04210 USA

toddlers
My busy day

by JILLIAN HARKER
illustrated by CAROLINE EWEN

Ten small fingers.

What can you do with them?

Two feet, ten toes.
It's fun to splash, to kick a ball,
or crunch through leaves!

Two bright eyes.
Have you seen
any of these?

One little nose.

Something smells good!

Two ears to hear music.
Which of these sounds have
you heard?

Two lips, one big kiss.

You can blow through your
lips as well.

A tongue for tasting.

Are these good to eat
and drink?

Have you ever done this?

There's lots to explore…

up and down, round and round.

Can you tell what's happening here?

There's so much to find out.

What a busy day!